An Unexpected & Unforgettable Adventure

Alice Parabia

Ukiyoto Publishing

All global publishing rights are held by

Ukiyoto Publishing

Published in 2024

Content Copyright © Alice Parabia

ISBN 9789361722462

All rights reserved.

No part of this publication may be reproduced, transmitted, or stored in a retrieval system, in any form by any means, electronic, mechanical, photocopying, recording or otherwise, without the prior permission of the publisher.

The moral rights of the author have been asserted.

This is a work of fiction. Names, characters, businesses, places, events, locales, and incidents are either the products of the author's imagination or used in a fictitious manner. Any resemblance to actual persons, living or dead, or actual events is purely coincidental.

This book is sold subject to the condition that it shall not by way of trade or otherwise, be lent, resold, hired out or otherwise circulated, without the publisher's prior consent, in any form of binding or cover other than that in which it is published.

This book is dedicated to my grandparents and parents

And the saga begins…

Foreword

Narration has been an integral part of the human psyche, for as far back as one can remember. Narratives have simmered in different cauldrons over time, adding to the vast expanse of stories around us; some that are carried from generation to generation and others that vanish into what we know as nothingness, only to reappear as dewdrops of wisdom or tiny tassles of gold dust, caught from the Sun as shimmering light sieves through dense thickets of foliage.

This reiterates the fact that storytelling comes naturally to many and if it starts early at a single digit age, then the sagcity that would perhaps emanate from it is indeed incomparable. This book is a roller-coaster ride along the brain waves of Alice Parabia, a young storyteller endowed with the unique quality of knowing exactly what she wants to say, how she wants to say it and the alacrity with which she eventually does so.

I have known this young versatile author since she was a little four-year-old, always eager to create her own stories and then share them. Innovativeness is her forte, with a dash of improvisation and her ability to see the extraordinary in the ordinary is what sets her apart in many ways. A bubbly kid with a very deep understanding of life, is how I see her. Mentoring her to complete this book has been one of the most rewarding experiences by far: But the question still remains who mentored whom? Some parts of the book have been kept the way she wanted them so as not to lose the essence, including play with words.

Suverchala Kashyap

Author of : Sunk in amber: dewdrops amidst rain
Of Long Forgotten Dreams a Kaleidioscopic feel

Contents

Rollicking Recess — 1
Lost in the woods? — 5
Dramatic Detour — 9

About the Author — *21*

Rollicking Recess

It was recess time at school and six best friends, who had made a group called the Spooky Shrills, as they liked spooky things, were always hanging out together. The girls' names were Alice, Sheya, Mrunal, Harvi, Avya and Ranvita.

One rainy afternoon they were walking on the school grounds and having a good time chatting at the top of their voices when suddenly they all slipped because it had been raining heavily and they went whoosh, whooosh…whhooosh, on the slimy mud and slid into a hole in an old banyan tree, which was full of sticky, gooey-gooey and stinky vines.

All of them screamed and shouted in terror, they were horrified as they slithered further and further into a dark, dingy hole in the tree. They couldn't see anything as it was pitch black and dark.

Sheya was trembling in fear as she often got terrified by the smallest things, but Alice the bravest of the Six Spooky Shrills said with complete confidence, "Don't worry everyone, we are all together, I'm sure nothing will happen! I am certain there is a way out of this strange place," said Alice with a brave voice.

Just then Mrunal said, "Hey look everyone I have a torch, as she fumbled to take it out of her school skirt's pocket" (then Sheya, Harvi, Avya, Alice, and Ranvita shouted to Mrunal) – "You could have mentioned this earlier, you know girl!" Just then they heard a ghostly sound as a gust of wind blew by them. Sheya said stammering and her teeth clattering, "*wwwwhhh...aat, wwaas eeeerrr, that, was it any of you playing a prank?* (The rest of them chorused, Nooooo, that was not us!)

As they sighed calmly Alice said, "Don't be such *scaredy cats*, that was just a normal natural sound at night perhaps." Perhaps! Sheya shouted. As soon as Sheya finished this sentence a thick fog appeared and a sharp breeze blew them all into three separate groups and far away from each other. They were stunned, Alice, Sheya, and Harvi were at the very tree they fell through: the old Banyan tree. Mrunal, Avya, and Ranvita were in the middle of the forest.

Alice, Sheya, and Harvi found a sign, which had the words faintly etched on it, 'Welcome to the **Spooky Ancient Enchanted Forest**.' Alice took command of the situation and blurted, "We better find Mrunal, Avya, and Ranvita quickly before we get into any trouble. Harvi gasped in fear, "but we don't know where they are, just look at it this forest is huge!"

As Alice decided to just walk around to see if she could find something to get them all out of this spooky little, *actually enormous* place, she spotted a weird-looking tree so she decided to take a closer look. She found a crumpled paper with a note attached to it written in *invisible ink*. She remembered reading about a riddle that would help anything written in invisible ink to show up...

The water is sometimes sweet and sometimes bitter, not from the sky and not from the earth. It suddenly struck Alice that the answer was *tears*.

How on earth would she find fresh tears, she thought to herself and as she looked around she saw Sheya crying as she was unable to get back home. Alice took the paper and ran to Sheya and collected her tears in a cupped thick leaf. Sheya had been crying for an hour and Alice managed to collect a whole lot of tears.

She gingerly poured the tears onto the crumpled paper and lo and behold! the map of the forest appeared in front of her. She takes a good look to see where they are stuck. It looked like they were stuck in the middle of the forest.

There was a wide stream of red liquid about 820 km from there and it seemed if they followed the stream they would find someone who could help them.

Apart from that something was glowing on the map and words appeared in a sentence that said *"If you follow the Red River you will find someone that you are looking for."*

4   An unexpected & unforgettable adventure

Lost in the Woods?

They all decided to follow the river and to their utter surprise, they found Mrunal, Ranvita, and Avya. They were all so happy to have found each other that they all started to cry tears of joy.

Just then Sheya started crying again as she realized that though they had found each other they were still lost in the woods. They were all extremely scared except Alice: her mind was not only racing but her heart was pounding with excitement, as she announced, "Look what I have, I have the map of the woods, that's how we found you." Everyone cheered and Sheya's tears almost went in reverse as she tried to put up a faint smile.

Mrunal exclaimed, "I'm very hungry…where could we get some food?" Alice said holding the map and studying it carefully, "Patience my friends, patience. Nothing comes easy, especially not in a forest. We have to walk nearly two kilometers to reach what looks like an orchard of absurd-looking fruits which are called 'dragon tears'".

"I will certainly walk with all of you but I am not going to eat anything to do with a dragon," said Ranvita. Oh! please, said Mrunal giggling it's just a fruit that looks like a dragon's tears and this is a forest with all kinds of creatures, so therefore it must be called a dragon tears' fruit. And by the way, "You never know it may be super delicious," pitched in Avya.

They walked, walked, and rested and walked again till they could walk no more but just then Alice, who was a little ahead of everyone, as she was leading with the map, looked over her shoulder and shouted, "Don't stop, don't stop, there's a terrifying looking creature up ahead, but it is fast asleep so we can tip toe across it and beyond."

Just as Sheya the *scaredy cat*, passes by the creature her foot accidentally touches the creature's tail and wakes it up. A deafening roar. Everyone got so terrified that Sheya fainted. The creature woke up and said, "Who dared to disturb my sleep?"

The girls screamed and then the creature screamed too, horrified with all the noise around it. The girls scampered up a tree as fast as they could and looked down and laughed because the creature was terrified of them. The creature said, "Are you here to kill me, just like most humans do?"

Alice replied, "Oh ! No, dear creature we just thought that you were going to harm us and eat us. We are lost in the forest and our parents must be so worried."

The creature shook himself up and said, "Don't worry girls my name is Doopey, and I am a friendly monster whose family has lived in this forest for generations. Sheya said, "Aaaa errr a MONSTER ?! She almost fainted for a moment again. She was so petrified and her heart was pounding so loudly that she felt it would pop out of her chest right into her hands. "Stop being so dramatic, Sheya, just for once try to be as brave as me," Alice murmured.

Doopey continued, "I can show you the way out of the forest, but it might take a few days or even months for that matter!" All the girls shouted together, "A few months!!!, you must be kidding, right?"

Doopey looked at them and said NOOOO, I'm not joking at all. Their jaws dropped; Sheya almost blacked out again. And Doopey whispered softly, "I am just joking , relax, stop being such drama queens."

Sheya looked towards Alice and said, "If I am such a big drama queen what about you?"

Alice replied assertively, "I am never a drama queen and by the way you do it every single second, at least I am just a drama queen once or twice a year." Everyone says Alice is right, you know Sheya.

Then Sheya started crying again, well wailing loudly with the words *I'm never right* echoing through the forest.

Alice suddenly realized that it was getting dark. So she announced, "C'mon folks, it is getting extremely dark and our parents must be getting worried about us and must be scolding our poor teacher Miss, Lily and our coordinator Ms Pathak and our Principal Mr. Thomas.

All too suddenly, just then Mrunal burst into a song and sang in her crackled voice:

8   An unexpected & unforgettable adventure

We are friends, friends forever:
we will never lose each other,
we will always be together.
We will face danger together,
we will always do things together.

Except for our personal stuff, err s...t...uff...

We laugh, we chuckle, we love each other.

We promise to never face danger alone,

We will never be alone as long as we are together.

Dramatic Detour

They started following the trail that Doopey showed them. Right now, happening in the real world the parents were shouting and screaming outside the school as they were very, very, angry and upset.

The Principal, the teachers, and the coordinator were very surprised and they knew that they were a team and they were all very good girls who loved adventure but they would never break any rules. So, the principal decided to check the CCTV footage, and what he saw shocked him. The girls had slid in the mud and fallen down a tree hole and all this during recess.

When the parents left the school, still worried about their children, Mr. Thomas called Mrs. Lilly and said, "Didn't you realize after recess during your class that some students were missing, they could be in danger.

Mrs. Lilly said, "I tried looking for them all over the school but couldn't find them and surprisingly all of them were not feeling well today so I thought they may have gone home after informing you, Sir."

"No, no, no Mrs. Lilly, you can't get away by saying just that. But Sir, I am telling you the truth," whispered poor, worried Mrs Lilly. I hope they are all fine she muttered under her breath as she left Mr. Thomas's room, her mind spinning and her heart beating very fast.

10 An unexpected & unforgettable adventure

Coming back to the forest the girls were on the right track with Mr. Doopey all along and were chattering away to distract themselves.

Mrs Lilly saw the place where they had disappeared and thought of writing them a letter and keeping it at that exact, same place.

She wrote,

"Dear Girls, everyone is very worried about you, please come back soon; where have you been? Everybody is finding you. I even got a scolding from Mr. Thomas and your parents as they are super worried about you all. Everyone is finding you, you just disappeared while sliding down a tree hole! Where are you my girls? Please write your message at the back of this paper as soon as you find it. I will be waiting. And I know you will certainly find it, eer at least I hope you will. I'm keeping my fingers crossed for you little girls and so is everyone else here."

Love Mrs. Lilly.

12   An unexpected & unforgettable adventure

She put the letter in an envelope and wrote over it from Mrs Lilly to Sheya, Mrunal, Alice, Avya, Ranvita and Harvi. Then she prayed to God and put the envelope through the tree hole. When it slid down there was a heavy breeze in the forest and the envelope flew straight to the girls.

The girls had taken a short break after walking for hours and decided to sit under a spooky but a vast canopied tree. They were actually quite tired but didn't want to admit it to each other. When they sat under the tree the envelope flew and landed on Sheya's head, as usual she shouted, as if a bullet had whizzed past her head.

"Calm down ! Calm down, said Alice, it's just an envelope. Let's take a look at what's inside?" They were absolutely shocked when they saw who the letter was from and they were stunned when they saw it was from Mrs. Lilly.

They read the letter and said, "Oh! No, our parents are worried and are scolding poor Mr. Thomas and Mrs. Lilly and if I know Mr. Thomas then he would have certainly scolded Mrs. Lilly.

Then Alice decides to ask Doopey, "Do you know a shortcut?" Doopey asked aloud,

" Can you give me the map I need to think." Alice gave him the map. Doopey looked at it and said, "I found a shortcut, but it is a little dangerous and I have not really mentioned this before but my family has been captured by a dragon and is kept captive in a cave and it is on the same path. If you help me to rescue my family I will lead you through the shortcut way. "

They kept walking through the trail that Doopey had shown them and then they came to two pathways, the one on the left was darker and the one on the right had a faint light.

Doopey instructed, "we have to go on the left side, Sheya was like, "Ohhh, I don't want to go on this side, I am sure it is terrifying." Alice retorted, "Don't worry Sheya, you can walk beside me all the way long and you will be fine."

Sheya replied, "Oh ! Fine Okay, but in case I get scared you have to carry me all the way. Then Mrunal, Harvi and Ranvita said, "Don't be such a drama queen! Learn to be brave like Alice. Alice said, "Alright, alright that's enough stop your blabbering, you guys…get real and by the way, I have already worked out a plan to defeat the dragon." Doopey said, "really Alice you did? You have it all worked out, really this is amazing."

Doopey softly informed that it would take an hour to reach the cave. Then Alice said, "Is it so?" I will explain it all on the way so that we don't waste any time as Mrs Lilly, the parents and Mr. Thomas must be getting worried sick by now. I hope our parents don't faint.

Alice continued saying that the plan is to approach the cave then Doopey will take us to the dragon and once the dragon realizes we are there, Mrunal, Harvi, Ranvita, Avya and I will distract the dragon, as we all know Sheya is the scaredy cat of the group and since

14 An unexpected & unforgettable adventure

Doopey knows where his family is so Doopey and Sheya will go sneakily to where Doopey's family is kept captured.

As they give us the signal that all is clear we will throw something so that the dragon runs after it and we quickly escape from the cave.

After an hour they reached the cave which looked scarier than the outside. As usual, Sheya got so terrified that she ran ahead of her friends behind the dragon with Doopey. While Harvi, Mrunal Alice and Avya were busy distracting the dragon, Sheya got the opportunity to free Doopey's family.

But then things took an unexpected turn, there was no family. Doopey was tricking them, once Sheya realized in that moment and Doopey said, "Hahaha I tricked you all, I am one of the servants of the dragon, as Doopey continued speaking Alice quietly defeated the dragon.

She had heard everything that Doopey had said when she had gone to find the gang then she hit Doopey with a big rock. Doopey was taken by surprise and fainted, after a while he woke and apologized to everyone and he was hypnotized by the dragon.

Sorry everyone, I am so sorry this happened, the dragon has been hypnotizing creatures for centuries. No one had been able to stop him from eating up anyone until now, you girls are so brave, you even defeated the dragon. Now all the creatures of this forest are free. Let me take you home.

But the path you came by is difficult, you came from a school and school is so boring how about you stay here with me and you can have the time of your lives. Then Alice said, "No Doopey, you are wrong, school is really fun, you get to learn many new things, you get to meet new friends: you have a lifetime experience: it's great fun in school.

It may look boring, but it's huge fun, you may faint if you go to school it's that fun. Doopey said, "Oh really, is that so?" Now even I want to go to school. Doopey was already excited about going to school, eating tasty food like French Fries, Chicken Manchurian, Pancakes Crepes with Nutella, Burgers and Chicken popcorn.

He was drooling, dreaming about such tasty food, when Alice just snapped him out by saying come on, come on, we need to move fast otherwise we will miss school and our parents will be so worried. Do you know how worried they will be Doopey?

Harvi asked Doopey, "Hey Doopey with all this talk about family, friends, teachers, schools, etc., where is your family, you haven't even mentioned a word about them before we snapped you out of the hypnotism of the dragon. That dragon is cruel, Mrunal said.

Alice said, "We can't leave you alone like this, so we will find your family before going home. Then Alice murmured, *"Only if we find them! I hope that we do soon, as I wanna get home quickly."*

If only there was a way to track your family down, Sheya said. Ranvita replied, "Well then before we start our search for your family Doopey, I am hungry, is anyone else, because I am STARVING girls and boy!

Then Doopey said, "Oh I know a tree that gives tasty but scary-looking fruits, and it's just one meter away. Then Sheya as usual drawled, "Scary looking fruits, errrr... they must be... errr... poisonous, as she fainted, falling with a huge bang as Doopey picked her up and said, Oh, No! what should we do ? May be we should take her under the tree and the fruit is known to be a remedy for anything and everything!

After that Ranvita said, "Oh no we must get to the tree as quickly as possible before she goes into her deep fainting spell for days, remember girls when that had happened. Oh! yes, Mrunal said, wasn't that in school when Mrs Lily called her for her good grades in class and she thought it was for bad grades and everyone laughed.

Mrunal again added, but I didn't laugh because I am a very good girl. Oh Yeah you were laughing said Ranvita with a grin. Didn't you girly?

Alright, alright said Alice, we need to get back home, let's hurry otherwise we will never reach home girlies!

As they started walking, they spotted a hole in the ground and Mrunal exclaimed, "Hey girls, this might be the way home !" Mrunal held Alice's hand then Sheya held Alice's hand and then Avya held Sheys's hand and then Harvi held Ranvita's hand and Doopey held Ranvita's hand and soon it became a chain of people frantic to get home.

Mrunal forgot that they had to first find Doopey's family. And then Mrunal jumped into the hole and entered into another dimension. Everything seemed so lovely and so beautiful as compared to the last ugly and dark one.

After that the girls said, "Wow this place is so mesmerising" (all chorused together). Alice suddenly spotted something written on a stone. "Oh! Look there is something written on this stone," Alice said adding, "It is written in some kind of ancient writing. Then Doopey said ", Let me take a look at it Alice please". Alice gave the stone to Doopey .

Then Doopey said ", This is the language of *Horror Wood*! I can translate it. Wait a second! This is my mother's handwriting!

Let me read it.

Alice said, "Wow! This sure makes things easy. Your parents were smart to have left this message.

An unexpected & unforgettable adventure

> Dear Son,
>
> We are in this new dimension, "We are trapped in a cave, as you know your father has the power of Teleportation, but this dimension is so strong that we can't get out of it by teleporting and if we get out we are only allowed for two minutes. So your father put this stone near the entrance for you to read. I have drawn a map at the back of this stone, it will help you to find us, but beware there is a monster guarding us because we are its slaves now. The monster's weak spot is it's stomach so you need to hit it on its stomach to make it faint and you can free us but there is a huge rock covering us so it will not be easy to get out. There is a puzzle before you fight the dragon, once the dragon faints, the rock will move.

"But hey, wait, it could also be a ploy to confuse us or to misguide us," said Alice wondering aloud after looking at the message carefully. Doopey turned the rock over and said " Come on let's follow the map to the cave." Sheya was so impatient to get home that she said to everyone, "What are we waiting for, let's Go, Go, GO Everyone, I want to get home now." Ranvita said, "Okay, Okay, Girl: we hear you loud and clear and we are doing it as fast as we can, you know?"

As they walked along their friendship grew stronger. Soon they reached the cave. They looked around the cave quietly so as to not startle the dragon. They found the puzzle, solved it, and went inside the cave sneakily,

without waking up the dragon. They reached Doopey's parents and got them out of the cave without waking up the dragon.

Once they got out of the dimension, Doopey hugged them and said, "I missed you both so much! We missed you too, Doopey's parents said together as they hugged each other. While they were all hugging the girls said, awwwwww.... isn't that cute? After that, Doopey's parents and Doopey escorted them to the exit of the dimension so they could get out.

20 An unexpected & unforgettable adventure

After they got out Mr. Thomas, Mrs Lilly and the girls' parents were waiting just outside the tree. They were jubilant on seeing their children and everyone hugged each other tightly. Mrs Lilly and Mr. Thomas asked the children how had they gone inside the tree? Then the girls said, "We were just walking and talking and suddenly we all slipped and there was a *whoosh* and we all landed on the other side through a tree." The girls said all together, "This was a crazy adventure."

Mr Thomas and Mrs Lilly left as they had some work to do, after that the girls told their parents together, we will tell you everything as soon as we get home because it is a very long story, but we will tell you after a very cosy, nice and sumptuous meal.

Then they all happily went home, okay folks I am done with this story. Hope you liked it?

Later that day they all met up and sat together and everyone except Sheya said, "So what will be our next adventure?" Then Sheya in a reluctant voice said, "Oh, No not another adventure, I need to lie down."

About the Author

Alice Parabia

Alice Parabia is an extremely intelligent, vivacious, curious and creative girl. She has a natural knack for storytelling, story writing, topped by composing poems and songs on almost any topic. Ever since she was a little girl, she has been dreaming of writing story books and publishing them. She creates stories with her vivid imagination: weaving magic around her. She has published a book with Bribooks too called, "The doll of my dreams." She has written this book with the support of SK's Transformational Hub also known as Parivartan with her mentor Suverchala Kashyap.

www.ingramcontent.com/pod-product-compliance
Lightning Source LLC
LaVergne TN
LVHW041643070526
838199LV00053B/3540